ASTRID LINDGREN

The Runaway Sleigh Ride

Illustrated by Ilon Wikland

Methuen Children's Books

First published in Great Britain 1984 by Methuen Children's Books Ltd, 11 New Fetter Lane, London EC4P 4EE
Reprinted 1985
First published in Sweden 1983 by Rabén & Sjögren Bokforlag, Stockholm under the title of *Titta, Madicken, det snöar!*
Copyright © 1983 Astrid Lindgren: English text copyright © 1984 Methuen Children's Books Ltd
Printed in Italy   ISBN 0 416 48200 7

One dark, wintry Sunday morning everyone at
Junedale was sleeping late. But soon they were all
awake. First Goodie, the cat, and Sasso, the dog, in the
kitchen, Alma in her room at the back, Mummy and
Daddy in their bedroom and Lisbet in her room – which
was Mardie's room too. Mardie wanted to go on
sleeping but Lisbet knew just how to wake her big
sister! She pulled up the blind with a crack.

"Look Mardie, it's snowing!"

Mardie leaped out of bed. The first snow – how
wonderful!

"I like it more than any other old snow," said
Mardie.

"Well I'd like all the snow in the whole world,"
declared Lisbet. Mardie laughed.

"What would you do with all the snow in the whole
world? We've got enough snow of our own."

And now it was falling thick and fast all over
Junedale. It made the birch trees round the house
white and beautiful and Mardie and Lisbet felt dizzy
and excited.

The two girls ran about in the snow all day.
They rolled in it, they made a snowman, they
built an igloo, and then they rolled in it again.
Sasso did too. He barked his head off he was so
happy. But Goodie just peered through the
kitchen window, thinking Sasso had gone mad.
She didn't understand snow. But
their father did and soon he ran out
to join them.

"I'll show you how I can knock
the snowman's nose off with this
snowball," he said. And he did too.

"I'll show you how I can
knock *your* nose off with this
snowball!" shouted Mardie.

So they had a snowball
fight. Daddy ended up falling
into a snowdrift but he didn't
mind, he roared with
laughter. At the kitchen
window, Mummy stood and
looked out – she thought he'd
gone mad too. *She* didn't
understand what fun snow
could be, any more than
Goodie!

The next day, Mardie had a temperature and had to stay in bed. What bad luck! She was to have gone Christmas shopping with Alma and Lisbet and afterwards they were going to make gingerbread with Mummy.

"I know someone who hasn't got a temperature," said Lisbet. "Now I can go with Alma all by myself and buy Christmas presents."

Mardie was angry. "You're horrid!" she said.

"Well, it's you I'm going to buy a present for, but maybe I won't if you're going to be so stupid!" said Lisbet.

"You and I'll go and buy Christmas presents another day, all by ourselves," said Alma, to cheer Mardie up. Mummy came to cheer her up too.

"Perhaps we can still make some gingerbread anyway. But you can't go walking round the town getting freezing cold."

"No, you must look after yourself," said Lisbet, coming over to Mardie and trying to tuck her in. But Mardie didn't want to be tucked in, especially by someone who hadn't got a temperature and was going Christmas shopping with Alma!

It was a wonderful day in town. All the shop windows looked so exciting. Alma and Lisbet walked round gazing at everything.

"It's nice being with Alma," thought Lisbet. "She never says, 'Come on, we've got to hurry!'"

"Come on, we've got to hurry!" said Alma just then. "We're going to the toy shop." But Lisbet didn't mind hurrying there; that's where she was going to buy Mardie's Christmas present.

Choosing took a long time. Lisbet would have liked to buy everything in the shop. Though maybe not *all* for Mardie.

"I'd love that for myself," she sighed, pointing to a sailor doll.

"Well, you'd better buy something for Mardie now, otherwise she'll have nothing on Christmas Day," said Alma, firmly.

So Lisbet bought a puzzle in a box for Mardie. On the lid was a picture of a kitten which had spilt a saucer of milk. Alma put the parcel in her bag.

"I'm sure Mardie will be pleased with that," she said.

"Yes, otherwise I'll have it myself," said Lisbet and Alma laughed.

"Oh, no! Now, you'll have to wait outside for a minute because I want to buy some things now."

"What sort of things?" asked Lisbet.

"It's a secret," said Alma. "Outside with you now! And don't go walking off anywhere, promise?"

Lisbet promised. She waited outside patiently and tried to peep through the window to see if Alma was anywhere near the sailor doll.

There were a lot of horses and sleighs in town today. Old farmers loaded
up with Christmas trees, birchwood, potatoes and apples; all things
to sell to the townspeople for Christmas. Suddenly, a sleigh appeared
from the square and Lisbet's eyes nearly popped out of her head when
she saw her friend, William, had sneaked a ride on the back runners!

"Bet *you* don't dare do this!" he called out to Lisbet as he passed by.

"Yes I *do* dare!" she called back.

"No you don't, you're just a little girl," cried William. And Lisbet
snorted. She was bigger than little William anyway! But the sleigh had
already carried him off into the distance. Soon another sleigh appeared
and stopped right outside the toy shop. The driver got out to deliver a
sack of wood to an old lady in the house opposite. She stuck her head out
of the window and shouted: "Here you are at last, Anderson!"

While Anderson was delivering the wood, Lisbet stood on the back
runners of his sleigh to see what it felt like. It didn't seem dangerous
at all. William needn't have been so cocky about it! But what *was* Alma
doing all this time? Was she buying up the whole shop? Lisbet craned
her neck to see if Alma was anywhere near that doll. Just then Anderson
came back. He patted his horse.

"Home to the farm, old girl!" he cried. And off they went.
But just as the sleigh moved, Lisbet hopped on to the runners
and stood there, just like William! Anderson didn't know
she was there, of course. He hadn't got eyes in the back of his head!

   "Oh dear, he is going a bit fast," thought Lisbet. "But I'll jump off the
next time he stops."

   But the sleigh moved quickly. Lisbet swished through the town
accompanied by the sound of sleigh-bells and felt marvellous.
What a shame little William couldn't see her now! But it would be nice
if Anderson stopped soon, before Alma had finished her shopping.

   But Anderson didn't stop. He was in a hurry to get home
to the farm and he had a long way to go.

   "Come on, old girl, get along there!" he said, waving his whip.

Lisbet wished she was at home now. She wanted to shout to Anderson to make him stop, but she didn't dare and he drove on and on. Soon they were far away from the town and Lisbet got very frightened. They passed several farms and each time she hoped it would be Anderson's. But it never was.

On and on they sped and soon they were in the forest. Nothing but snowy fir trees everywhere. Lisbet wished she'd never jumped on the horrible sleigh. It never stopped, not even when Anderson drank from his bottle. He still drove with the reins in one hand and the bottle in the other! And he began to sing:

> *"Here there's drinking to be done,*
> *Blow it all, it makes life fun!"*

He sang other things too that were even worse. But Lisbet couldn't bear it any longer.

"Stop!" she yelled. "I want to get off!"

Anderson turned his head and saw her. And at last, the sleigh came to a halt. Anderson was angry.

"Have you been there all the way from town?"

"Ye−es," cried Lisbet. "And now I want to go home!"

"Well, you'd better get a move on then," said Anderson. And Lisbet cried even harder.

"Yes, but you'll have to *take* me!" she sobbed.

"That's what you think! Nobody asked you to jump on my sleigh. There's the road! Start walking!"

And he drove away, leaving Lisbet standing there. She heard him start singing his horrible song again, but soon there was nothing but silence in the wood. No singing, no tinkling of sleigh-bells. Just the faint whispering of the wind in the trees.

"Now I'll just die," thought Lisbet. Alone on a snowy road in the middle of the forest so far from home. She started to run. She ran and ran for all she was worth. But it wasn't easy, running and crying at the same time and soon she had to stop. She stood in the snow, sobbing and called:

"Mummy, Mummy! Where are you?"

But Mummy couldn't hear. She was just about to start making gingerbread, back at home in Junedale.

"I don't know *where* they can have got to all this time," she said to Mardie. "We can't wait any longer, we'll have to start baking!"

"They must be buying up the whole town before they come home," said Mardie. She felt better now and was looking forward to the baking. Mummy had made two large lumps of gingerbread dough, one for Mardie and one for Lisbet. Mardie started making gingerbread animals in long rows. But without Lisbet, it wasn't as much fun as usual and she couldn't wait for her sister to come rushing in, crying: "Have you started already?"

Then Alma came back. Alone. Poor Alma, she'd looked everywhere for Lisbet.

"Is Lisbet here?" she cried anxiously. And when she found out Lisbet wasn't, she cried so hard the tears gushed out of her eyes.

"She promised not to walk off anywhere," she wailed. Mummy went quite pale when she heard the full story.

"Where on earth can the child have got to?" And she rang Lisbet's father at work.

She turned to Alma. "Come on, we'll have to go back to town and look for her."

"But I have already!" said Alma, as she sat among the baking tins, crying.

Meanwhile, Lisbet was struggling through the snow-drifts. The road never seemed to end! And why did it have to snow so hard! Lisbet was angry. How could she have said she'd like all the snow in the whole world!

"Not this horrible snow, though! And not any other snow, either!" she sobbed. She was so angry it made her push her way through the snow more easily, but she was miserable and tired and hungry and all alone. How could everything be so dreadful?

"Mummy!" she cried. "Mummy, where are you?"

Then suddenly she saw a cottage a little way off the road, in the trees. Surely there would be some kind person who could help her? But there was no one at home. And then Lisbet cried so hard her whole body trembled. Poor little girl. If her mother could have heard her then, she would certainly have cried too!

Next to the cottage was a small cow-shed. Perhaps there were people in there? Lisbet banged on the door. She heard such a bellow from inside that she jumped. Maybe they only kept angry bulls in their barn? But Lisbet wanted to get warm inside so she tried the door. It wasn't locked. What luck!

Inside, a cow stood alone in its stall. She bellowed even more loudly when Lisbet walked in. But she soon quietened down and looked at Lisbet with kind cow-eyes.

Lisbet patted her cautiously. Just a cow! So, she wasn't quite alone in the world, after all.

It was nice in the cow-shed and there was some straw in an empty stall, so Lisbet lay down to sleep for a while. But very soon she woke up, shivering. She patted the cow and warmed herself a little against her side. But then she went out into the snow again.

"I must get home soon, or I'll just die! Stupid old Anderson!" she shouted to herself.

She trudged through the snow struggling and crying, a little bit at a time. But finally, she was so tired she stumbled and fell by the side of the road. It was the last straw!

"That's it! I'm not getting up any more!" she shouted to the trees.

But Lisbet knew it was dangerous to lie down in the snow, unless you dug yourself in to stop yourself from freezing to death. So she tried tossing some snow on to her stomach. But it didn't help much.

"The way it's snowing now, I'll be buried soon anyway," she thought. "Oh, how I hate Anderson!"

Then suddenly she heard singing and the tinkling of sleigh-bells coming nearer. Was it just old Anderson coming back? But no, it wasn't Anderson at all, it was another farmer and his wife driving their sleigh to town. Lisbet jumped up and shouted with all her might:

"Oh, please, can you give me a ride?"

"Goodness, child," said the woman when she saw Lisbet standing like a snowman by the side of the road. "What *are* you doing out here all alone in the forest?"

But Lisbet burst into tears and couldn't answer. So the farmer jumped down from his sleigh, brushed the snow off Lisbet's clothes and lifted her up on to his wife's lap.

"There, there, it's all right now," he said. And it certainly was, as the farmer's wife wrapped her warm shawl round Lisbet, tucked her feet in under the sheepskin rug they had over their knees, and took off her wet mittens to warm her hands in her own. She held her tight, very tight, in her arms. It was really wonderful, but Lisbet cried all the same. Eventually, she stopped sobbing to tell them what her name was and where she lived and why she was so far from home.

"Oh, you poor little thing," said the farmer's wife, over and over again. And her husband urged his horses on through the snow.

"Don't cry now, we're taking you home to your mother."

And the farmer and his wife began to sing again, as they always did when they were out in the sleigh:

> "Now that the daylight fills the sky,
> We lift our hearts to God on high,
> That He, in all we do or say,
> Would keep us free from harm today."

Lisbet sighed. It was so nice sitting in the warm, gliding along in the sleigh while it got darker and darker in the forest and hearing the singing and the bells tinkling and nothing else. Soon she fell asleep and she slept until the sleigh stopped at the gate to Junedale.

Inside, in the kitchen, Mardie sat alone
with Goodie and Sasso, waiting and waiting.
Mummy, Alma and Father, with lots of
other people, were out looking for Lisbet.

It was completely dark now and Mardie
was getting more and more worried. What
if they never found Lisbet, what if she never
came back, what would happen then?

"I suppose I'll have to make her gingerbread too," thought Mardie. But it didn't
feel as if it would be much fun. Mardie
started to cry. Oh, how she wished Lisbet
was there!

"Lisbet, where *are* you?" she called, just
as if Lisbet could hear her!

And just then the door opened and there *was* Lisbet!

"Here I am," she said, laughing.

Mardie rushed up and threw her arms round her and they hugged and hugged each other for a long time. At last Lisbet said:

"I want something to eat!"

"You can have a sandwich," said Mardie. And she pointed to the kitchen table where there was bread and butter and milk and cheese and cold meatballs. Mardie spread butter on one slice of bread after another. Lisbet couldn't get enough. She ate and ate so much she could hardly answer when Mardie asked her:

"But where have you *been* all day?"

"I've mee niding wian ig alled Anderson," said Lisbet through her sandwich. But Mardie understood straightaway that she was saying, "I've been riding with a pig called Anderson"!

While Lisbet told the whole story, Mardie looked at her reproachfully.

"You promised Alma you wouldn't go walking off anywhere!"

"Well, I didn't," said Lisbet, thinking carefully for a moment. "I *rode!*"

Mardie hugged her again. "You are bad! But I'm glad you're back."

Mardie let Lisbet try her gingerbread and tomorrow she would make her own. But soon Lisbet was tired and yawning.

"I know what we'll do," said Mardie, "we'll go to bed. And when Mummy and Daddy come home, there'll be *two* children lying there instead of one. Just think how happy they'll be!"

Lisbet nodded: "Yes, because there's a big difference between two children and only one!"

There was no time to lose to get into bed quickly so that Mummy and
Daddy wouldn't get home first and spoil the surprise.

"Will you put your arm round me?" asked Lisbet.

"Yes, of course I will!" Mardie could think of nothing better.
"Because do you know what? When Mummy and Daddy come home and
want to say goodnight to me, they'll see your empty bed and they'll cry."
They giggled with delight at the thought of their mother and father
crying when there was no need at all. "And then – woosh! – you stick
your head up from under my bedclothes and say: 'What are you crying
for?' They'll laugh and laugh!"

Lisbet giggled again. Then she sang the song she had just learnt:
> *"Now that the daylight fills the sky,*
> *We lift our hearts to God on high,*
> *That He, in all we do or say,*
> *Would keep us free from harm today."*

"Where did you learn that?" asked Mardie. And Lisbet told her.

"But Anderson, that pig, sang one too!"

"Sing it then," said Mardie.

Lisbet shook her head. "No, I mustn't!"

But Mardie insisted: "Oh, go on, sing it!"

"Under the bedclothes then," said Lisbet. And they crept under the
covers and Lisbet sang very softly:
> *"Here there's drinking to be done,*
> *Blow it all, it makes life fun. . . ."*

Then she stopped. "I shouldn't sing any more, should I?"

"No, it's bad," said Mardie, "but sing it just once more, anyway."

But Lisbet wouldn't. She burst into *Now that the daylight* again instead.
Then Mardie suddenly remembered something:

"Just think, what if I've given you what I've got and you get a
temperature too?"

"It doesn't matter," said Lisbet. "I'm not going out tomorrow,
anyway." Then she thought for a moment.

"I'm not going out again before Christmas. And maybe never!"
Mardie was amazed. "Why not?"

"I've been out enough," said Lisbet.

Mother and Father and Alma came home shortly after. And they were
so unhappy that they couldn't even cry. But they went up to the
children's room to say goodnight to Mardie. And in Mardie's bed they
found two small girls lying there close together, fast asleep.

Lisbet's mother and father stood there looking at them. They held
each other's hands and tears trickled down their cheeks.

"Thank heavens," whispered Mummy. "Thank heavens!" Because
there certainly *is* a difference between two children and only one.

Happy Christmas, Mardie and Lisbet!